Chapter 1

"Wow!" Katie Carew exclaimed as she stepped onto the Mermaid Sea cruise ship for the first time. "This is amazing."

Katie felt like she had just walked onto a magical floating palace. She'd never seen anything like it. The walls were painted gold and silver, there were huge, crystal chandeliers shimmering from the ceiling, and the windows were framed with deep-red, velvet drapes.

"This place is gorgeous!" Katie said.

"The crystals on that chandelier match my earrings," Katie's best friend, Suzanne Lock, told her. She pulled back her dark hair to give Katie a better look.

Katie tried not to laugh. Suzanne was always finding new ways to show off the fact that she had pierced ears. Katie's ears weren't pierced. At least not yet. But she wasn't in any hurry. Pierced ears were more a Suzanne kind of thing than a Katie kind of thing.

"I'm so glad we decided to take this cruise together," Katie's mom told Suzanne's parents. "The girls will have so much more fun this way."

Katie nodded. That was for sure. It was a lot more fun to go on vacation with a friend. Being around adults all the time could get pretty boring.

"I know! I can't wait until we dock at that island in the Caribbean Sea," Katie said. "We get to swim with dolphins! I've never met a dolphin before."

"Of course not," Suzanne said. "Where would you meet one? It's not like you have a dolphin in your class or anything."

"That's because dolphins don't swim in

schools. Fish do," Katie's dad joked.

Katie giggled. Her dad told the worst jokes. But he was right: Dolphins weren't fish. She'd learned that during her class's learning adventure about mammals. Her teacher, Mr. G., had dressed like a cow that day. And he'd explained that there are all kinds of mammals— like cows, monkeys, cats, dogs, people, and dolphins.

"I heard there are a lot of really great stores on the island," Suzanne said. "Didn't you tell me that, Mom?"

Mrs. Lock nodded. "There's definitely plenty of shopping."

"Boat! Boat!" Suzanne's two-year-old sister, Heather, shouted suddenly. She squirmed around, trying to get out of her father's arms. But Mr. Lock held her tightly.

"She's going to be a pain in the neck," Suzanne whispered to Katie. "I hope we don't have to spend all five days of this cruise babysitting Heather."

Katie didn't think Heather was a pain in the neck. She thought she was kind of cute. Of course, that was probably because Heather wasn't Katie's little sister. Katie figured having her around all the time was probably harder than it looked.

"Mom, Heather has a stain on her collar already," Suzanne complained.

Mrs. Lock sighed. "That happens to babies."

Suzanne spun around so the skirt of her sailor dress flew up around her. "My dress is always clean," she said. "I'm a very careful eater."

Katie rolled her eyes. There wasn't anything Suzanne couldn't—or *wouldn't*—brag about.

Just then, a woman in a blue dress walked over to where the Carews and the Locks were standing. She smiled at Katie and Suzanne.

"Welcome aboard," she greeted them. "I'm Lori, the head counselor at our Cruisin' Kids

Club. I bet I'm going to see a lot of you guys over the next five days."

Katie grinned. She'd read all about the Cruisin' Kids Club in the brochure. It looked great. There were so many activities.

"Is there really an ice-skating rink on this boat?" Katie asked Lori excitedly.

Lori nodded. "And a rock climbing wall, a waterslide, basketball courts, and a miniature-golf course."

"Wow!" Katie said. "I can't wait to skate in the middle of the ocean."

"I brought my ice-skating skirt. It's in one of those bags over there," Suzanne said. She pointed to the huge pile of suitcases the Locks had brought for the cruise. Suzanne wasn't the only one in her family who liked to change outfits a lot.

Lori smiled. Then she looked over at Heather. "This must be your little sister," she said to Suzanne. "She looks so adorable in her sailor dress."

Uh-oh. Katie frowned. Lori shouldn't have said that. Suzanne really didn't like when anyone got more compliments than she did.

"Hers has a stain on it," Suzanne pointed out angrily. "And it's too big on her."

"She'll grow into it," Lori said sweetly.

"We're not going to be in the same group as Heather, are we?" Suzanne asked.

Lori shook her head. "Heather will use our babysitting service. You two will be in the Cruisin' Kids Club's Minnow group. That's for third- and fourth-graders only."

"Thank goodness," Suzanne said.

"Boat! Boat!" Heather squealed again.

"Yes, Heather," Suzanne's dad said. "We're on a boat."

"She's adorable," Lori said.

"She's a *pain*," Suzanne whispered to Katie. "And she's going to ruin my trip. I wish we had just left Heather at home."

Katie gulped. Suzanne had just made a wish. That was *sooo* not good.

Wishes could bring big trouble, especially if they came true. And no one knew that better than Katie.

Chapter 2

It had all started back in third grade on one
terrible, horrible, miserable day. First, Katie
had missed catching the football and lost the
game for her team. Then she'd fallen in the mud
and ruined her favorite jeans. And then she'd
stood up in front of her whole class and let
out the biggest, loudest burp in the history of
Cherrydale Elementary School. *A real record
breaker.* Talk about embarrassing.

That night, Katie had wished that she could
be anyone but herself. There must have been a
shooting star overhead when Katie made her
wish, because the next day the magic wind
arrived.

The magic wind was a wild, powerful tornado that blew only around Katie. It was so strong that it was able to blow her right out of her own body and into someone else's. One . . . two . . . switcheroo!

The first time the magic wind came, it turned her into Speedy, the class hamster. Katie spent the whole morning stuck in a cage, going around and around on a hamster wheel and eating wooden chew sticks. When she finally escaped from the hamster cage, she'd wound up stuck in somebody's smelly gym sneaker. *P.U.!*

Katie was really glad when the magic wind returned later that day and changed her back into herself. But that wasn't the end of the magic wind. It came back again and again. And every time, it changed Katie into somebody else.

One time she turned into her classroom snake, Slinky—and shed her skin, right on the classroom floor. Talk about an itchy situation! You don't know what an itch is until you itch your skin right off your back.

And how could Katie ever forget the time that the magic wind switcherooed her into a famous baseball player named Mike Reed? Mike was an awesome shortstop. But Katie wasn't. She dropped a really important fly ball—and then started to cry. Only the fans didn't know that it was a fourth-grade girl who was crying. They thought a major leaguer was having a major meltdown. And it was all caught on the jumbotron!

And then there was the time Katie turned into Suzanne's hairdresser, Sparkle, on the day of Suzanne's big modeling show. Katie had to cut Suzanne's hair—and oh boy, what a disaster that had been. Suzanne wound up with long hair on one side, short hair on the other side, and a big mess on top!

As far as Katie was concerned, wishes brought nothing but trouble.

"Don't worry about Heather," Katie told Suzanne. "We'll hardly see her. We're going to be hanging out with kids our own age at the Cruisin' Kids Club."

"You certainly will," Lori assured her. "But first we have to have our lifeboat drill. And then we're off to sea."

A little while later, Katie and Suzanne were on the Pool Deck of the ship. From up there, the girls could see for miles and miles. The ship had begun to move out to sea. New York City's harbor was getting smaller and smaller.

Suzanne waved her hand and blew kisses. "Good-bye, good old USA," Suzanne called to the people on the dock. "Don't worry, I'll be back."

Katie giggled. Suzanne was always so . . . so . . . *Suzanne*!

Instead of blowing kisses, Katie pulled out the new camera her grandmother had bought her just for the cruise. Katie's grandma was in Cherrydale watching Pepper, the family's cocker spaniel. But Katie had promised to take lots of pictures.

Katie looked through the viewfinder on her camera. She was just about to snap a picture of the dock when suddenly Suzanne stuck her face right in the middle of the shot.

"What are you doing?" Katie said. "You ruined my picture."

"No I didn't," Suzanne told her. "I made it better. Pictures with people in them are so much more personal than just plain pictures. A picture without a person might as well be a postcard."

"I just want a picture of the sign that says *New York City* as we sail away from the dock," Katie told Suzanne.

"So I'll point to the sign. You're lucky, Katie Kazoo," Suzanne said, using the way-cool

nickname Katie had gotten from her friend George last year in third grade. "Some models charge a lot to be in pictures. But I'm posing for you for free."

Actually, Suzanne wasn't a real model. She was just a fourth-grader who took modeling classes. But Katie didn't say that. She didn't want to start arguing with her best friend now. Not when they were about to go on a five-day vacation together.

So Katie snapped a picture of Suzanne pointing to the sign. Then she watched as New York City got farther and farther away. Before long she couldn't see any land at all. There was nothing but bright, blue-green seawater all around.

Katie's cruising adventure had begun!

Chapter 3

"Whoa! Look at this!" Katie exclaimed excitedly as she and Suzanne entered the Cruisin' Kids Clubhouse. The clubhouse overlooked the Pool Deck. All the walls were made of glass. "We can see everybody in the pool from here!"

"And they can see *us*," Suzanne said. She went over to the window and smiled. Then she tossed her hair back over her shoulder and pushed one hip out to the side.

Katie thought Suzanne looked pretty silly. But she knew her best friend was trying to be all model-y, so she didn't say anything.

"Oh, great! Here are two more Minnows,"

Lori said as she walked over and handed Katie and Suzanne each a lime-green wristband. "You guys need to wear these all the time," she explained. "That way we know you're members of the Cruisin' Kids Club."

Suzanne looked down at the green wristband and made a face. "Can I have a purple one instead?" she asked. "Purple is a much better color for me."

Lori shook her head. "All the Minnows wear green wristbands," she explained. "The purple wristbands are for the Guppies. They're the kids who are in first and second grade."

As Lori walked away to greet some more kids, Suzanne sighed. "See? Little kids get all the good stuff. We get the leftovers. Like these ugly, green bands."

"I *like* green," Katie told Suzanne. She fastened her bracelet around her wrist and smiled.

Just then, another girl with a green wristband walked shyly over to Suzanne and

Katie. "Are you Minnows, too?" she asked, twirling her long, brown hair around her finger nervously.

Katie smiled and held up her wrist. "Yep," she said. "I'm Katie, and this is my best friend, Suzanne."

"I'm Lizzie." The girl smiled shyly at Suzanne. "I love your sailor dress."

Suzanne twirled around so the skirt of her dress ballooned all around her. "Thanks," she said. "I got it especially for the cruise."

"I got my shirt especially for the cruise, too," Lizzie said. She pointed to her yellow tank, which had a purple starfish in the middle.

Katie could tell Lizzie was waiting for Suzanne to tell her that she liked her shirt, too. But Suzanne didn't say anything. Katie wasn't surprised. Suzanne loved getting compliments—she didn't always like to give them.

So Katie said, "That's really cute. I love starfish."

"Me too," Suzanne said. "Maybe I'll get starfish-shaped earrings on the island."

"I don't have pierced ears yet," Lizzie said. "But my mom said I could get them pierced next year when I'm in fourth grade."

Suzanne was about to say something when suddenly Lori made an announcement. "Can

I have all my Minnows over here by the door? We're off to have some fun."

Katie smiled. No one liked fun more than Katie Kazoo!

"So? Are we going to the rock wall or the basketball court?" a Minnow named Stan asked as the group walked up the stairs to the next level of the ship. At least Katie thought his name was Stan. He could have also been his twin brother, Dan. They looked so much alike, it was really hard for Katie to tell them apart.

"Why do you think we'll start off doing one of those things?" Katie asked him.

Dan said, "We've been in a whole lot of these Cruisin' Kids Clubs, and it's always the same."

"I've never been on a cruise before. Not ever. I mean not once!" a girl named Carly said really fast. "I couldn't wait to go on this one, though. I saw all the pictures and I just knew it was going to be the most fun I ever had. *Ever.* I mean where else can you . . ."

"Do you think she'll ever stop to take a breath?" Suzanne whispered in Katie's ear.

Katie giggled. "She's just excited," she told Suzanne. Katie was trying to be nice. But Suzanne was right. Carly was still talking even though no one was listening anymore.

"We're going rock climbing!" Lori said excitedly.

Katie had never been rock climbing before. But she was really excited to try.

"How are you going to rock climb in a dress?" Lizzie asked Suzanne.

"No problem." Suzanne smiled and lifted up a corner of her dress. "I'm wearing shorts underneath. So I can do sports and still be stylish."

"Wow!" Lizzie seemed really impressed.

Katie wasn't all that impressed, though. Suzanne had been doing the shorts-under-her-skirt thing since the beginning of third grade. She'd been bragging about it since then, too.

As they reached the top of the stairs, Katie

spotted the rock wall. It was a tall, gray wall that had been painted to look as though it were the side of a steep cliff. There were red, yellow, and blue knobs sticking out all the way up. Katie figured those were the places you were supposed to put your feet as you climbed.

"Who wants to go first?" Lori asked the kids.

Katie looked over at Suzanne. She figured Suzanne would volunteer just so she could brag about being the first Minnow to reach the top. But Suzanne didn't raise her hand. She just stood there looking up at the top of the wall.

So Katie raised her hand. And the next thing she knew, she was strapped into a harness and hooked up to a rope.

"Okay, Katie, now all you have to do is reach up and grab on to one of the yellow or red handholds," Lori told her. "You can use them to pull yourself up. And as you pull, put your feet on the green or blue footholds. Then keep on climbing."

Katie frowned. Lori made it all sound so easy.

But it was really, really hard. It took a lot of strength to pull herself even a couple of feet up the wall.

"Come on, Katie, you can do it," Lori cheered.

Katie wasn't so sure. The wall was really tall. And that just made her feel really, really small.

"Whoa!" Katie shouted as her body swayed from the wall.

"It's okay," Lori said. "You're connected to the safety rope. You can't get hurt. Just grab that yellow handhold. And put your foot on the blue knob to your left."

Katie Kazoo was no quitter. She reached to her right and grabbed on to the yellow knob, just like Lori had told her to do. She pulled herself up and rested her foot on the blue knob. Then she pulled herself higher and higher and higher still. And then . . .

Ding! Ding! Ding! Katie reached up and rang the bell at the top of the rock wall.

Woo-hoo! She'd made it!

"Yay, Katie!" Lori called from below.

Some of the other kids clapped.

Katie grinned. She felt like a real mountain climber—if there were a real mountain out in the middle of the ocean somewhere.

"Okay, let yourself dangle and we'll pull you down," the man working at the rock wall said.

So Katie jumped out a step. A moment later she was back down on the deck of the ship.

"Great job!" Lori said. "Who wants to be next?"

Carly raised her hand. "I'll do it. I think I can reach the top. At least I hope I can. It might be tough because I'm not that strong but . . ."

Katie laughed. She wondered if Carly was going to talk all the way up the wall. Carly stopped talking, though, as she got higher up.

Before long, all the kids had had a turn except Suzanne. She was still staring up at the top of the wall.

"Don't you want to try?" Lori asked her.

"It's really, really high up," Suzanne said. "I sometimes get dizzy when I'm up really high."

"It's not that high," Stan said. "Not like a real mountain."

"Come on," Katie said. She pulled her camera from her pocket. "I'll take your picture."

That made Suzanne smile. A little.

"Okay," she said. "I guess I'll climb. After all, models have to be willing to pose anywhere."

A few minutes later, Suzanne was slowly making her way up the wall. She put her foot on a green knob and pulled herself up with a blue one. Then she put her foot on a red knob and reached for a green one.

Katie pointed her camera at Suzanne and clicked a photo just as Suzanne lost her footing and started to fall. *"Aaahh!"* she screamed. "Get me down from here."

The man who was working at the rock wall quickly lowered her down.

Katie ran over right away. "Are you okay?" she asked.

Suzanne nodded. "You can't ever show anyone that picture. I didn't have a chance to smile."

Chapter 4

"Now this is more like it," Suzanne said as she and Katie took their seats with the other Minnows in the middle of a row in the crowded auditorium. "A magic show. Do you remember when I was George's assistant when he put on a magic show at Mandy's birthday party?"

Katie did remember. She'd never forget it. How could she? Suzanne had ruined every one of George's tricks. But Katie didn't remind Suzanne about that part.

"You were a magician's assistant?" Lizzie asked her excitedly. "Onstage and everything?"

"Well, it wasn't really a stage. We were at a

party," Suzanne explained to her. "But it was still a real magic show."

"Wow!" Lizzie said. "So you're a model *and* a magician's assistant."

Suzanne smiled. "Exactly."

"Shhh," Katie said. "The magic show is starting."

"Hello, everybody!" the magician shouted as he ran out onto the stage. "I'm Marvin the Magnificent. Are you ready to have some fun?"

"Yes!" the kids in the audience answered.

"Great," the magician said. "Now, for my first trick, I will need a helper from the audience."

Lots of kids put their hands up. But Suzanne put her hand up the highest. She started bouncing up and down in her seat. "Me! Me!" she shouted. "Pick me!"

Marvin the Magnificent stepped down from the stage into the audience. The closer he got, the higher Suzanne bounced. And the louder she shouted, "Me! Me!"

Marvin stopped right near Suzanne and Katie. He smiled. And then he reached out and pointed right at *Katie*.

"How about you?" he asked her. "Would you like to be my assistant for this trick?"

Katie didn't know what to say.

Suzanne, on the other hand, had plenty to say. "Why her? She has no experience."

That made Katie mad. Why did Suzanne
always have to be picked for everything?

So Katie said, "Sure. I'd love to."

Katie didn't even glance at Suzanne as she
walked onstage.

"Okay, now I want you to hold this empty
hat," Marvin the Magnificent said as he and
Katie stood before the audience. "Show everyone
that there's nothing in there."

As Katie held up the hat for the audience,
she noticed some movement in the row she
had been sitting in. Suzanne was storming
out of the auditorium. Lizzie was following
right behind her.

But Katie wasn't going to let Suzanne ruin
her fun. She smiled at Marvin the Magnificent
and handed back his hat.

"So, do you like birds?" he asked Katie.

Katie nodded. "Are you going to pull a bird
out of that hat?"

"Not yet," he said. "Can you say the magic
word?"

"Abracadabra!" Katie shouted.

"Actually, I asked you to say *the magic word*," the magician told her.

Katie giggled. She knew what he meant.

"The magic word," she repeated.

The magician grinned and reached into the hat. He pulled out an egg. "That's almost a bird," he joked. "Now say that other magic word."

"That other magic word," Katie repeated.

"No," Marvin the Magnificent told her. "I meant *abracadabra*."

Katie laughed. Marvin the Magnificent was really funny. "Abracadabra!" she exclaimed.

The magician cracked the egg into his hat. He took a fork and beat the egg like he was making scrambled eggs. Then he reached into the hat and pulled out a beautiful, white dove.

"Wow! How did you do that?" Katie asked.

"A magician never reveals his secrets," Marvin the Magnificent told her. He put a gold-colored medal around her neck. "Thanks for your help."

"You're welcome," Katie told him. As she walked off the stage and back to her seat, she looked down at the medal. It had a picture of the cruise ship on it. It was really cool. Katie decided she was going to wear it all day long. She didn't care at all what Suzanne might say about it.

Chapter 5

"Nice medal," Suzanne said that evening as the two families sat down at their dinner table in the Caribbean Sunset dining room.

Suzanne didn't sound like she really liked the medal at all. In fact, she sounded like she was mad at Katie for wearing it.

"Did you see my new earrings?" Suzanne asked everyone. She pulled back her hair and showed off her orangey-pink coral earrings that were shaped like roses. "I got them on the Promenade Deck. There are jewelry stores, clothing stores, and a souvenir shop. There's a hair and nail salon, too. Just like Sparkle's

Salon. It's like a mini Cherrydale Mall. Only prettier."

"Do they have a candy store like Cinnamon's Candy Shop?" Katie asked excitedly. "Or a pizza place like Louie's?"

Suzanne shook her head. "There are no food shops on the Promenade Deck."

"I guess they figure there's enough food here in the dining room," Katie's dad said. "Have you guys taken a look at this menu? There are so many things to choose from. I'm thinking of ordering one of everything."

"You'd end up with one big stomachache," Katie told him.

"Probably," her dad agreed. "Or just one big stomach."

Katie giggled. Her dad was so funny.

"Cookie!" Heather shouted suddenly. "Cookie!"

"No cookies until you eat dinner," Mr. Lock said. He looked down at the menu. "How about some nice macaroni and cheese?"

"Cookie," Heather repeated.

Suzanne rolled her eyes.

"I'm starving," Katie said. She looked at the section of the menu that said VEGETARIAN DELIGHTS. "Mmm. They have personal-sized pizzas with vegetables."

Suzanne pulled her hair back even farther and shook her head so everyone at the table would look at her earrings again.

"Those earrings are lovely, Suzanne," Katie's mother complimented her.

"She just had to have them," Mrs. Lock explained. "She seemed so upset about not being able to be in the magic show. But I knew these would cheer her up."

"They're real coral," Suzanne boasted. "Lizzie helped me pick them out. She and I had a great time on Deck Five. I like her a lot. I know we're going to spend a lot of time together on this cruise."

Katie frowned. Suzanne was making it sound like Lizzie was her new best friend or something. Even though Katie knew she was acting that way because she was mad about the magic show, it still hurt.

"Did you see the way they folded the towels in the bathrooms of our cabins?" Katie's mom asked everyone.

"Ours was shaped like a monkey," Katie said. "When I came in, it was hanging from the light fixture. It was so cute."

"Ours was an elephant," Suzanne told everyone. "They had to use three towels to make it. It was huge."

"I wonder how they do that," Mrs. Lock said.

"They're giving a whole class on towel folding," Katie's mother told her. "Right after dinner in the Clamshell Lounge."

"Oh, maybe Lizzie and I can go together," Suzanne said. "I bet she would love to learn how to make a towel elephant."

Katie tried not to feel bad when Suzanne mentioned Lizzie's name. But it was really tough. Especially because Katie knew Suzanne was doing it on purpose. Still, Katie felt better a little while later when their waiter, Mario, placed a pizza with vegetables in front of her. It smelled delicious.

"I asked the chef to put extra mushrooms on it," Mario told her.

"Thanks," Katie said. She picked up a slice of pizza and took a bite. *Mmm.* It tasted even better than it smelled.

For a while, Suzanne forgot about being mad. She seemed happy to be eating her spaghetti with clam sauce and talking about all the cool stores on the Promenade Deck.

But just as Mario brought Katie her slice of chocolate pudding pie, Lizzie came walking over to the table. "Hi, Suzanne," she said. "I love your pink dress."

Suzanne smiled. "I wore it to dinner because it matches my new earrings."

"Are you going to play miniature golf tonight with the other Minnows?" Lizzie asked her.

"I was going to go to the towel-folding class instead," Suzanne told her.

"Oh." Lizzie looked really sad. "My mom said I have to go with the club. She doesn't want me wandering around the ship without a counselor."

Suzanne shrugged. "Well, I guess we could go play mini golf for a little while."

Lizzie smiled so widely, Katie thought her teeth might pop out of her mouth. "Really?" Lizzie asked excitedly. "Oh, I'm so glad! You're so nice, Suzanne. I'm so glad I met you."

Suzanne laughed. "I hear that a lot," she said.

"I'm a very good friend."

Katie giggled. Suzanne wasn't wrong. She *could* be a very good friend. Especially to herself. In fact, there wasn't anything Suzanne wouldn't do for Suzanne.

Chapter 6

The next morning, the ship had docked in the island harbor. But Suzanne was in a very grumpy mood. Everything seemed to make her angry.

"That was the worst miniature golf," Suzanne complained as the Locks and the Carews walked down the gangway. "It took me forever to get the ball into those little holes."

Katie figured Suzanne was mad because last night she had gotten the worst score of all the kids in the Minnow group. It had been a hard miniature-golf course. In fact, Katie had done pretty badly, too. The only kids who got decent scores were Stan and Dan. But they'd played on a lot of cruise ship mini-golf courses.

Still, Katie wasn't upset about anything. How could she be? She was on a beautiful island with palm trees and sunshine. And soon she would be arriving at Dolphin Reef, the park where she and her parents could swim with dolphins.

What could be more exciting than that?

"I smell the sea!" Katie exclaimed happily.

"So what? That's all we've been smelling since yesterday," Suzanne reminded her.

"But it smells better here," Katie said. She sniffed at the air. "Mmm. Something smells like coconut, too."

"That's my sunscreen," Suzanne said. "I bought it in a shop on the Promenade Deck."

"Tree!" Heather said. She pointed up to one of the palm trees. "Pretty tree."

Katie smiled. "The palm trees *are* pretty, Heather," she told Suzanne's little sister.

"Lizzie and her family are going on a special tour of the island," Suzanne said. "They're going to get coconuts right off of palm trees. And they're going to get to crack open the coconuts and drink the milk."

"That sounds like fun," Katie said. "But not as much fun as swimming with a dolphin. I wonder what my dolphin's name will be. I bet we get to be buddies this afternoon."

Suzanne frowned. "Only *you* would want to be friends with a fish," she said.

Katie wasn't going to let Suzanne ruin her day. "Dolphins aren't fish," she told her. "They're mammals, just like us."

"Well, I don't want to spend all day in the water," Suzanne went on. "My skin will get all prunelike. And my hair will be a mess."

Katie sighed and didn't answer.

"There's the sign for Dolphin Reef," Katie's mom said. "That's where we're supposed to go."

She pointed toward the end of the dock. Katie could see part of a small enclosure. There were lanes like in a swimming pool. Katie's heart started beating a little faster. This was so exciting! Any minute now she'd be face-to-face with a real, live dolphin!

Chapter 7

"Welcome to Dolphin Reef. I'm Steve, your guide on your dolphin encounter. I'll be introducing you to your new dolphin buddies. Today you will all be hanging around with Flippy and Flossie. I know you are going to love them."

Katie was so excited, she could barely sit still on the dock as Steve explained all the fun things she was going to get to do with Flippy and Flossie.

"After you put on your life jackets, I'm going to lead you down to the water where you will each get to step out onto a platform in the water and meet your new dolphin friends," Steve explained. "The dolphins are very friendly. In fact, I'm sure that after a few minutes, at least one of them is going to want to give you a big kiss."

Suzanne groaned. "Just what I need—a kiss from someone with fish breath," she said. "Why couldn't we have gone to the coconut grove with Lizzie and her family?"

Katie pretended she didn't hear Suzanne. Instead, she asked Steve, "How will we know which dolphin is Flippy and which is Flossie?"

Steve pointed to his right arm. "Flippy has a black spot right in the middle of his right fin. He's hard to miss."

"Kind of like a freckle," Katie said. She had a few freckles herself.

"After you get a kiss, Flippy and Flossie will take each of you on a speedy ride down one of the lanes! The dolphins will push your feet until you stand and soar through the water."

"Is that okay with the dolphins?" Katie asked. "I mean, what if a person is too heavy for them to push?"

"Flippy and Flossie are very strong," Steve assured her. "These dolphins are very, very well cared for. We love our dolphins, and they are treated much better than most working animals. Nothing you do here today will hurt them. I promise."

Katie was glad to hear that. She would never hurt an animal. Ever.

"Just how long is our swim with the dolphins?" Suzanne's father asked.

"Each person will get fifteen minutes to swim with the dolphins," Steve told him. "But you are free to spend all day at Dolphin Reef Park, looking at our other wildlife and enjoying our beautiful beach."

"Only fifteen minutes?" Katie asked. This was the first thing all day that did not make her happy. "Why so little time?"

"It's hard work for the dolphins," Steve

explained. "They take a break every hour for a rest and a fishy treat."

"I work longer than that on my science homework," Katie murmured under her breath. "And I don't always get a snack after I do my work. Boy, dolphins have it really easy."

"Okay, everyone. Let's put on life jackets," Steve said.

Katie wanted to take a picture of her parents in their big, yellow life jackets. But she had left her camera in a bag back in one of the lockers by the dock.

"May I go get my camera?" Katie asked her parents. "I'll be back in a flash."

"Sure. Our stuff is in locker 427," her mother said. "But hurry. You don't want to miss out on all the fun!"

"I'll hurry," Katie promised. "I can't wait to play with the dolphins—even if it's just for a little while."

Katie inspected the row of lockers, looking for 427. It was in the back by the curtain-covered changing area.

Suddenly Katie felt a cool breeze blowing on the back of her neck. It wasn't a gentle, ocean-smelling tropical breeze like she had felt when she'd gotten off the boat and stepped onto the island. This was stronger and colder.

And then the breeze picked up speed, which was strange because there weren't any windows

or fans in the dressing room. Even weirder, the curtains in the locker room weren't moving a bit. In fact, the wind didn't seem to be blowing anywhere except around Katie.

Katie gulped. That could mean only one thing. This was no ordinary wind. This was the magic wind! It had followed Katie to the island!

"Oh no!" Katie shouted. "Not now. Not when I'm about to swim with a dolphin!"

But the magic wind didn't care about swimming or dolphins. It just kept spinning around Katie. Faster and faster it whirled, blowing cold air all around her. Katie shut her eyes tight and tried not to cry.

And then it stopped. Just like that. The magic wind was gone.

And so was Katie Kazoo. She had turned into someone else. One . . . two . . . switcheroo!

But who?

Chapter 8

Katie could hear waves lapping around her and seagulls flying overhead. In the distance she could hear laughter.

Slowly, she opened her eyes and looked around. She was surrounded by blue-green water. The sun made the water look like it was full of shimmering diamonds and turquoise.

Okay, so now Katie knew where she was—in the water. But she still didn't know *who* she was.

She looked down at her feet. But Katie didn't see her sneakers. She didn't see her sandals. She didn't even see toes.

All she saw were two large fins. One on each side of her gray-white belly. Katie was so surprised, she sent a huge stream of water right out of her blowhole.

Wait a minute. Fins? Gray-white belly? Blowhole?

You don't usually find those on a fourth-grade girl. At least not any fourth-grade girl Katie had ever met.

Katie looked down at her right fin. There was a big, black freckle in the middle of it. That could mean only one thing—the magic wind had switcherooed Katie into Flippy, one of the Dolphin Reef dolphins!

There was the dock. From where she was swimming, Katie could see her parents alongside Suzanne and her whole family. They were waiting to have a dolphin encounter. And not just with any dolphin.

They were waiting to meet Katie! Only they had no idea it was her.

This was *sooo* not good!

"Fishy!" Katie heard Heather shout excitedly.

"Not fish. *Dolphin*," Katie shouted up from the water. Well, that was what Katie tried to say, anyway. The only thing Heather and the other humans heard was a bunch of squeaks and squeals. Dolphin noises.

"How about you go first?" Katie heard Steve ask Suzanne.

"I don't know if I want to get kissed by a dolphin," Suzanne said. "They look slimy."

That made Katie mad. She wasn't slimy at all. She was wet and shiny.

"Where's Katie, anyway?" Suzanne asked. "She's who wanted to get a dolphin kiss."

"She went to get her camera," Katie's mom told her. Katie gulped. She wished she could tell her mom that she was right there in the water!

"Come on, Suzanne," Mrs. Lock urged. "I'd love to get a picture of you being kissed by a dolphin."

"Our photographer is standing right there, ready to shoot," Steve told Mrs. Lock.

"A photographer?" Suddenly Suzanne seemed excited. "Okay, then. I guess just one kiss wouldn't hurt." She turned to the woman with the camera. "Can you shoot me from my good side?" she asked.

"Which side would you like?" the photographer asked her.

Suzanne thought for a minute. "I guess it doesn't matter," she said finally. "We models can make it work from any angle."

Katie laughed so hard, she snorted.

"I think Flippy likes you," Steve said. "He sounds happy."

Suzanne smiled. "Animals do like me."

Katie rolled her dolphin eyes. *Oh, brother.*

"Flippy, it's your turn to kiss the kid," Katie heard someone say. She turned her dolphin head slightly. Another dolphin had popped up out of the water right beside her. That had to be Flossie.

Katie definitely did *not* want to kiss Suzanne. Not the way she'd been treating her.

Suzanne had been a real pain ever since that magic show.

"Can't you kiss her?" Katie squeaked to Flossie.

Flossie shook her head. "It's your turn."

Katie sighed, which made a blast of air whoosh through her blowhole. There was no getting out of this one. She was going to have to swim over and give Suzanne a big old smooch.

Katie had learned to swim at sleepaway camp last summer, but she had never done the dolphin kick—until now. Of course, it helped that Katie was a dolphin! With a few flips of her side and back flippers, she sailed through the water.

"Wheee!" Katie squealed happily as she swam. "This is fun!" She leaped up and twirled around in the air.

"What was that for?" Flossie asked. "Are you showing off for a better treat? It's not worth it. We haven't had squid in weeks. Just fish, fish, fish."

Oops. Katie hadn't meant to show off. She

was just showing everyone how much fun it was to whiz through the water. Quickly, she dived down in the water. A big wave washed up onto the dock as Katie's tail splashed back.

"Oh no!" Suzanne shouted. "My hair! It's all wet."

Uh-oh. Suzanne didn't like getting her hair wet. She worked too hard on making it look perfect. Now there was a big piece of seaweed hanging off the side of her head.

Katie felt so bad about what she had done that she leaped up and gave Suzanne a big kiss on the cheek.

Click! "I got the picture," the photographer said. "Who's next?"

Suzanne leaped up from the platform. She glared at the photographer. "I can't believe you took my picture when my hair was a mess! I HATE THAT DOLPHIN!"

Chapter 9

Katie was sorry for Suzanne, and she was sorry for Flippy, too, because the rest of the tourists didn't want him kissing them. Everyone wanted kisses from Flossie.

And every time Flossie gave a kiss she got a treat. By the time Flossie had kissed Katie's dad and mom and Suzanne's parents, she was plenty full. But Katie's stomach was completely empty. No treats for her.

She was determined to fix that. Even though Katie was a vegetarian, Flippy wasn't. And it was Flippy's belly grumbling with hunger. So Katie decided to make sure that belly got filled with fish.

"Now it's time to go for your rides," Steve announced. "Which of you brave souls is ready to be propelled by dolphin power?"

"Not me," Suzanne said. "I just dried off."

"I'll give it a try," Katie's mom volunteered, and she jumped into the water. "Oh, I hope Katie gets back here soon or she's going to miss this."

"Just float on your stomach with your arms and legs apart," Steve said. "Flossie and Flippy will do the rest. We call this the foot push."

Uh-oh. Katie had no idea what "the rest" was. She looked over at Flossie. "What did he mean?" she asked.

"Are you kidding?" Flossie bleated back. "You know what to do. We perform this act ten times a day."

"Right," Katie said nervously. "Of course. I was just testing to see if you remember how we do it. Do you?"

"Quit kidding around," Flossie said.

"I already have a bellyache from all those fish. You'd think they'd try a different treat once in a while. A little squid or octopus meat would be nice."

But Katie wasn't focused on food. Her mother was already floating on her belly not far from where Katie and Flossie were. Flossie started swimming toward Katie's mom.

"Come on," Flossie shouted back to Katie. "Didn't you see the signal?"

No. Katie hadn't seen any signal. So she just followed Flossie. After all, she was a real dolphin. She'd be able to show Katie how this foot push thing went.

Flossie began swimming faster and faster toward Katie's mom. So Katie began to swim faster, too.

Whoosh! The seawater flew across Katie's dolphin skin. She took a deep breath through her blowhole and kicked her fins even harder.

Katie was swimming really fast. So fast

that she couldn't stop. There was no brake on her fins.

Katie was heading straight for the side of the pool.

"Runaway dolphin!" Suzanne shouted.

But Katie's mom couldn't run. She couldn't swim very well, either, in her big, yellow life vest. Katie didn't want to risk bashing into her mom. So she used her back fins to turn her mom around.

The water began to spin like a giant, twirling, swirling whirlpool.

"Whoa!" Katie's mother shouted as she spun around like a pinwheel. She went under and then came back up coughing.

Oh no! Quickly Katie swam over and scooped her mom up onto her snout.

"You're safe now, Mom," Katie said. "I rescued you."

But Katie's mom didn't know what Katie was saying. All she heard was dolphin squealing and squeaking.

Thump. Bump. Mrs. Carew's rear end bounced up and down on Katie's snout. "Get me off this dolphin!" she shouted. "It's like a bucking bronco."

"Put her down, Flippy!" Flossie cried out. "She's not a beach ball."

Katie spun around again, looking for a safe place to put her mom. Water splashed everywhere.

"Tidal wave!" Suzanne shouted.

"Put her down!" Flossie ordered.

"Get me off!" Katie's mom yelped. It was all too much. All that shouting and yelping was hurting Katie's sensitive dolphin ears. And so she did what any dolphin would do. She dived underwater where it was nice and quiet.

"WHOOOOAAAAAA!" Mrs. Carew flew off Katie's snout and into the air. *Splash!* She landed right on her belly in the water. A perfect belly flop.

"Are you okay, Mom?" Katie cried out as she came back up to the surface. Of course,

Katie's mom didn't understand a word she was saying.

"Mom?" Flossie asked Katie. "Who are you calling *mom?*"

Oops. Katie had completely forgotten she was a dolphin for a minute there.

But Steve hadn't. He thought Katie was Flippy.

"Get Flippy into the isolation tank immediately," Steve called to one of the trainers. "Let him cool down. And keep him away from the visitors."

★ ★ ★

A few moments later, Katie found herself all alone in a roped-off section on the far side of the dock. She was really embarrassed and sad. Worse yet, everyone thought it was Flippy who had messed everything up.

Suddenly Katie felt a cool breeze blowing across her dorsal fin. She looked around. The sea was perfectly calm. The palm trees in the distance weren't swaying at all. The clouds in the sky weren't moving. In fact, there didn't seem to be wind blowing anywhere—except around Katie.

That could only mean one thing: This was no ordinary wind. This was the magic wind. It was back!

The magic wind picked up speed, blowing faster and faster like a wild, windy whirlpool around Katie. Even though she was a big, heavy dolphin, Katie was sure the wind would blow her clear back to the harbor in New York City. Faster and faster it spun, sending seawater all around her like a whirlpool. Katie shut her dolphin eyes and tried not to cry.

And then it stopped. Just like that. The magic wind was gone.

Katie Kazoo was back! And so was Flippy. He was floating in the water right beside Katie. Boy, did he look flipped out. He had absolutely no idea why he was in the isolation area of Dolphin Reef.

But Katie couldn't explain it to him even

if she wanted to. She was a fourth-grade girl again. And fourth-grade girls don't speak dolphin.

Chapter 10

"Katie! What are you doing in there?"

Suddenly Katie heard Steve calling to her. She looked up from the water and smiled. "Hi, Steve," she said.

"You shouldn't be here by yourself," he said. "And you shouldn't be alone with Flippy."

"Why not?" Katie asked. "He seems really sweet."

"Well, he is, usually," Steve said. "But Flippy is an animal. And animals are unpredictable. He's done some very strange things today. I'm wondering if maybe his days of swimming with guests are over."

Oh no! Katie felt terrible. She knew that none

of what happened was Flippy's fault. It was all her fault. But of course she couldn't tell Steve that. He wouldn't believe her even if she did. Katie wouldn't have believed it, either, if it hadn't happened to her.

Katie scrambled back up onto the dock. She shook her head. Water flew out of her hair as if she had a blowhole up there.

"Flippy flipped your mother in the water," Steve said. He shook his head. "I don't get it. He usually follows directions perfectly. After all, he knows he'll get a treat if he does the right trick at the right time."

Katie made a face. "You mean those little, squishy fish?"

Steve laughed. "Dolphins love those little, squishy fish."

"Are you sure about that?" Katie asked. "Maybe if you gave him a different treat, Flippy would do anything you told him to."

"Well, we do have a little bit of squid in the refrigerator," Steve said slowly. "It's worth a try.

At least I'll see if he's ready and willing to do his tricks."

A few minutes later, Steve arrived back at the isolation area with some squid meat.

Katie reached down into the water so she could pet Flippy. Flippy gave her a big dolphin smile and jumped up to gently place a kiss on her cheek.

"Perfect," Steve said. He gave Flippy a piece of squid. Katie didn't have to speak dolphin to understand how happy that made him.

"Okay," Steve said after Flippy did a few

more tricks. "You want to try a foot push with Flippy and Flossie?"

"Definitely!" Katie exclaimed.

★ ★ ★

"Okay, Flippy and Flossie are ready!" Steve called out to Katie a few minutes later when they had all arrived back at the main pool. "Just get on your belly with your feet spread apart."

Katie's dad was focusing her camera and clicking away.

A moment later, Katie felt two dolphins pushing at her feet. She stayed on her belly for a moment, and then she began to stand. *Whoosh!* Katie flew through the water with Flippy and Flossie at her feet.

"This is awesome!" Katie exclaimed. "I—"

But Katie didn't finish her sentence. Instead, she fell face-first into the water. But Katie didn't mind. She knew that was part of the fun. Sort of like falling down when you were waterskiing.

"That was good," Katie's dad said. "You were up a pretty long time. I got some good shots."

Katie smiled. She was really proud of that.

As Katie climbed out of the pool, Steve had Flippy and Flossie do all kinds of tricks: flip around in the air, balance balls on their noses, and even speak—well, at least speak like a dolphin. It was all bleeps and pings and squeals to Katie.

"My dog, Pepper, can bark on command," Katie told Steve. "I just have to give him a cookie as a reward."

Steve grinned. "It's amazing what animals can learn when you train them with treats."

"With the *right* treats," Katie pointed out.

Steve laughed. "Have you ever thought of being a dolphin trainer one day?" he asked Katie. "You understand them so well. It's almost like you've gotten right inside Flippy's head."

Katie giggled. That is *exactly* what it was like.

Chapter 11

"Is that skating outfit real velvet?" Lizzie asked Suzanne the next morning as the Minnows all gathered by the ship's seaside skating rink.

Their first activity of the day was to go ice-skating. Katie loved skating. But she'd only been skating in the winter at outdoor rinks. It would be cool to go skating indoors aboard a ship!

Suzanne seemed really excited to skate as well. Or at least she was excited to *dress* for skating.

"*Of course* it's real velvet," Suzanne told Lizzie. "And I made sure my mom got me a purple velvet one. Purple velvet is just so royal-looking."

"You do look like a princess," Lizzie said. She looked down at the jeans she was wearing. "I wish I had brought a skating skirt."

"I think it makes me look so much more professional," Suzanne agreed.

"Oh, it does," Lizzie assured her.

"Isn't it cool to be going skating on a ship?" Carly asked Katie. "I've only been skating a few times but it was really hard for me. I fell a lot. I can't imagine what it will be like if the ship starts rocking back and forth while I'm on the ice. That's going to make it even tougher to skate. I wonder if I'll fall this time. Maybe if I stay near the wall and go really slowly . . ."

Katie tried to look as though she were really interested in what Carly was saying even though she wasn't. Carly talked a lot but never said much. Still, Katie wasn't the kind of person to be rude. Not like Suzanne. Right now, she and Lizzie were standing really close to each other, whispering and ignoring all the other Minnows. Katie couldn't understand why they were being so snobby.

"This skating rink is really cool," Stan told Katie.

"No, it's really cold," Dan joked.

Katie giggled. "That's how skating rinks are supposed to be."

Stan nodded. "Definitely," he agreed. "The rink on this ship has real ice. Not all of them do."

Suzanne turned around. "That's ridiculous," she said. "All ice-skating rinks have ice."

Dan shook his head. "The cruise ship we took to Mexico had plastic ice."

Suzanne rolled her eyes. "Yeah right," she said. "You two think you know everything about cruise ships."

Just then, Lori walked over. "Are you all ready to skate?" she asked the Minnows.

"Is there such a thing as a skating rink with

plastic ice?" Suzanne asked.

"Not on *this* cruise line," Lori assured her. "But other cruise ships do have synthetic rinks. They are plastic."

"See?" Stan and Dan said to Suzanne.

Suzanne didn't answer. Instead, she twirled around and let Lizzie admire her skating skirt again.

"Okay, everyone," Lori said cheerfully. She threw open the doors to the rink. "Let's skate!"

⋆ ⋆ ⋆

A few minutes later, Katie had her skates laced up, and she was on the ice. She was surprised at just how much skating on an indoor rink inside a cruise ship felt like skating outside at the Cherrydale Rink. It was still cold, and the ice was still wet. And Katie's rear end still hurt when she fell.

"That's the third time you've fallen," Suzanne said as she watched Katie pull herself up off the ice. "I haven't fallen once yet."

Katie knew that was because Suzanne

hadn't moved away from the rail. She was just standing there, smiling as the other kids skated by.

"Come on, Suzanne," Lizzie called to her. "Skate with me."

Suzanne didn't answer her at first. Katie could tell she was hoping Lizzie would go off with someone else.

"I don't think Suzanne knows how to skate," Dan said.

Stan agreed. "Suzanne doesn't do any kind of sports."

Katie wanted to see how Suzanne was going to react to that. Stan had practically dared her to skate. Katie knew Suzanne could never refuse a dare.

"Oh yeah?" Suzanne said to Dan and Stan. "Watch this." And with that, she started skating around the ice. She skated slowly at first, and then she picked up speed to try to keep up with Lizzie.

"See?" Suzanne asked Stan and Dan. "I can

skate as well as anybody. It's not hard. You just put one foot in front of the other and . . . WHOOPS!"

Boom. Suzanne landed with a thud.

"Ouch!" Suzanne exclaimed. "This ice is hard. And cold."

Suzanne crawled over to the rail and picked herself up. The back of her skirt was all wet.

At just that minute, Suzanne's parents and baby Heather arrived. They wanted to see the girls skate. Heather took one look at Suzanne's wet rear and started to giggle.

"Suzanne, wet," she said. "Suzanne, diaper."

"I DO NOT NEED A DIAPER!" Suzanne shouted back at her little sister.

Everyone skating at the rink stopped and stared at her. "Well, I don't," she grumbled angrily as she stormed out of the rink. "*Sheesh.*"

Chapter 12

"I am sick of sports," Suzanne grumbled as the Carews and Locks were eating dinner in the cruise ship dining room. "It's all we ever do in that stupid Cruisin' Kids Club. Today we played HORSE on the basketball court, and then we had those silly relay races in the pool. Why would anyone expect me to be able to push a ball down to the deep end with my nose?"

"I thought the relay races were fun," Katie said.

"Yeah, but you don't care about looking like a fool," Suzanne said. "I can't do that. You never know when you're going to run into someone from a modeling agency. What if there's an agent right here on the boat, and he saw me pushing a ball with my nose? He'd never hire me."

Katie doubted there was anyone who worked at a modeling agency on the cruise ship. But Suzanne had been acting so mean during this whole cruise, Katie didn't really feel like talking to her about this or anything else.

"I don't know why we can't do something really fun," Suzanne continued. "Like sing karaoke at the karaoke café. I could sing a Bayside Boys song. I bet everyone would love to hear that."

Katie wasn't so sure. She'd heard Suzanne sing.

"The karaoke café is just for grown-ups," Suzanne's mother told her.

"Oh. Well, I don't need a café to do karaoke."

Suddenly Suzanne stood up and began to sing. *"If you go, I'll miss you. If you stay, I'll kiss you. Cause you're my girl, girl."* She stopped and looked at everyone at the table. "See? I had a lot of fun doing that. Don't you think the kids in the club would love it?"

The Carews and Locks just stared at her. No one knew what to say.

"Uh, sure," Katie said finally. "Karaoke is always fun."

"I'll bet you girls are excited about the midnight chocolate buffet," Katie's dad said. Then he smiled at Suzanne. "That has nothing to do with sports. Unless eating has become a sport."

Suzanne and Katie giggled.

"I'm definitely excited!" Katie exclaimed. "Only I can't decide."

"Decide what, Kit Kat?" her mother asked her.

"If I'm more excited about eating all kinds of chocolate or about being allowed to stay up past midnight," Katie answered.

The grown-ups all laughed.

"I've been up past midnight before, haven't I, Mommy?" Suzanne boasted.

"I don't remember that," her mother replied.

"Sure you do," Suzanne said. "That time we went to see the Christmas show at the Cherrydale Arena. We got stuck in all that traffic on the way home and didn't get home until midnight."

"Oh, right," Mr. Lock said. "It was before Heather was born. You fell asleep in the car, and I had to carry you inside."

Heather perked up at the sound of her name. "Me," she said. "Me."

"No, Heather," Suzanne told her little sister. "We were talking about *me*." She turned her attention back to her dad. "I woke up when you were carrying me," Suzanne reminded him. "And that was after midnight. So that counts."

Suzanne's dad laughed. "I guess so," he agreed.

"Maybe I'll pass on dessert at dinner," Katie's mom said. "Save my sweet tooth for the chocolate buffet."

"The ship hired a chocolate artist from

France to carve all the sculptures," Mrs. Lock told everyone. "His name is Chef Pierre Éclair, and apparently he can carve just about anything from chocolate. From the pictures I saw, some of those statues could be in a museum."

"Chocolate statues?" Katie asked excitedly. "Wow! That sounds like my kind of museum."

"Mine too," Suzanne agreed. She thought for a minute. "I wonder if Chef Pierre needs a model for his statues. The statues in the Cherrydale Art Museum are all based on real artists' models."

"I think the chocolate statues here are mostly of fish and whales and dolphins," Suzanne's mom told her. "Things you see in the sea. It's a cruise, after all."

"I guess that makes sense," Suzanne said.

"Oopsie!" Heather exclaimed suddenly. She looked down at her lap. There was pizza all over her flowery dress. "Pizza, bye-bye."

"Oooh! Gross!" Suzanne shouted. "Heather,

you are such a pig!"
"Want pizza!"
Heather shouted.
"More pizza." She
started to cry.

"Suzanne, can
you cut one of your
slices of pizza in half
and give her some?"
Suzanne's mom
asked.
"Why should I
have to do that?"
Suzanne asked.
"It's not my fault
she's a pig."
"More pizza!
More pizza!"
Heather wailed.

"Suzanne, please," her mother pleaded. "Just
share the pizza. It's easier to compromise with
Heather than listen to her cry."

"I am sick of sharing and compromising!" Suzanne grumbled as she cut a slice of pizza for her little sister. "There isn't one thing on this cruise that's just for me. I'm really sick of it! Something around here has to change!"

Uh-oh. Katie didn't like the sound of that. That sounded like trouble.

Chapter 13

But Katie wasn't thinking about trouble when she, Suzanne, and Lizzie walked into the main dining room at midnight. All she could think about was chocolate!

"Wow!" Katie exclaimed. "This is amazing!"

Everywhere she looked in the dining room she saw chocolate. White chocolate swans. Milk chocolate dolphins. Dark and white chocolate whales. They were beautiful.

"I can't believe my mom and dad are at a show," Lizzie said. "Who would want to miss this?"

"Our parents are at the show, too," Suzanne told Lizzie. "But that's over by twelve thirty.

They'll get to eat plenty of chocolate."

"Boy, I wish Cinnamon could see this," Katie said. "I thought *her* candy store was magical. But this is incredible."

"It's like walking into a game of Candy Land," Suzanne agreed.

"Didn't you love that game?" Lizzie asked Suzanne.

"I did," Suzanne said. "And I was very good at that game."

Katie bit her lip and tried not to laugh. Being good at Candy Land wasn't hard. It was all luck. "Ooh, I'm dying to taste that white chocolate," she said, trying to change the subject.

"Oh, you'll have to wait for zat," a man in a white coat and a chef's hat said with a French accent.

"Why?" Katie asked. "Isn't this the midnight chocolate buffet?"

"Eet eez," the man said. "But for zee next hour, people are only allowed to take peectures

of zee chocolate." He smiled at Katie. "Take out your camera. Make a memory."

But Katie didn't take out her camera. "A whole hour?" she asked the man in the hat. It was so late, and she was so tired. "But by then it will be one in the morning. And I'm tired already. I don't know if I'll be able to stay awake that long."

"That's because you wore yourself out doing sports all day," Suzanne told her. "I told you karaoke would have been better."

"Well, I guess I can wait up if it means I can try some of that chocolate whale," Katie said.

"Oh, we do not actually cut up zee sculptures," the man in the chef's hat said. "We refrigerate zem and use zem as decorations for zee rest of zee cruise. Only zee small candies and pastries are for eating. You can have chocolate tarts right after I, Chef Pierre Éclair, feeneesh carving a sculpture in zee chocolate."

"*You* are Chef Pierre Éclair?" Suzanne asked him.

Chef Pierre Éclair stood a little taller. "*Oui.* Zat eez me."

Suzanne gave him a look. "You talk funny," she said.

Chef Pierre didn't answer. Instead, he turned and walked away, mumbling something in French under his breath.

As Chef Pierre left, Katie frowned. "Pastries? That's no big deal. They served those same pastries for dessert at dinner tonight. I already had a chocolate tart."

Just then, Carly came running over.

"Hi!" she said. "Are you guys here to see the

chocolate-carving demonstration? Chef Pierre is about to carve something out of a big block of chocolate. Right here. In front of everyone. I wonder what he'll make. Do you think it will be a fish? Or a sea anemone? Or a mermaid? Oooh. I hope it's a mermaid. I love their tails and the way they—"

"It seems so unfair to have all this yummy chocolate around just to look at," Katie complained. She yawned. "I'm just going to go back to my cabin and go to sleep."

"Katie's just not used to staying up late," Suzanne told Lizzie and Carly. "But midnight is *early* for me."

Carly and Lizzie looked really impressed.

"Come on," Suzanne continued. "Let's go look around at all the sculptures."

As Suzanne and the other girls strolled off, Katie headed for the stairs. The hallways were completely empty. Everyone on board the ship seemed to be at the show or the midnight chocolate buffet.

Suddenly, Katie felt a cool breeze blowing on the back of her neck. She looked around. Funny. There were no open windows in the hallway and no air-conditioning grates.

So where was that wind coming from?

Suddenly the breeze began to blow faster and colder until it was no longer a breeze at all. It was a full-fledged wind. A whirling, twirling tornado of a wind that was blowing just around Katie.

Uh-oh! This was no ordinary wind. This was the magic wind! It was back. And it was really, really strong. So strong that Katie thought it could blow her halfway across the ocean!

Katie was cold, tired, and really, really scared. She shut her eyes tight and tried very hard not to cry.

The wind blew stronger, whipping Katie's red hair around her face and blowing the skirt of her blue dress up and around her. Harder and harder it blew, and then . . .

It stopped. Just like that. The magic wind

was gone. But so was Katie Kazoo. She had turned into someone else. One . . . two . . . switcheroo.

But who?

Chapter 14

Slowly, Katie opened her eyes. She looked down. Her red high-top sneakers were gone. They'd been replaced with a pair of white shoes. She wasn't wearing her blue dress anymore. She was wearing white pants and a white shirt.

She was still on the ship—otherwise she might have thought she'd turned into the ice-cream man who drove down her block in the summer in his big truck.

Not only was Katie still on the cruise ship, but she was back at the midnight chocolate buffet. Everywhere she looked, passengers were smiling at her.

Okay, so now Katie knew *where* she was. But she still didn't know *who* she was.

"And now, ladies and gentlemen, our own Chef Pierre will carve a beautiful flying fish from this block of dark chocolate," someone suddenly announced over a loudspeaker.

Katie looked around to see where Chef Pierre was. A thousand eyeballs stared right back at her.

Okay, how weird was that?

Katie looked away. Then she looked back. All those eyes were still focused on her. That was when Katie noticed the giant block of dark chocolate on the table in front of her. There were all sorts of fancy knives and carving tools beside the chocolate.

Uh-oh. That could only mean one thing: The magic wind had turned Katie into Chef Pierre—just before he was supposed to carve the chocolate into a flying fish.

The only time Katie had ever carved anything was back in summer camp. She'd used a plastic knife to carve some white soap into the shape of a flower. It hadn't gone very well. And now all these people were expecting her to carve a beautiful flying fish out of chocolate in front of their very eyes!

This was *sooo* not good!

Katie wanted to run out of the dining room as fast as she could, which would have been a very fourth-grade girl thing to do.

The only problem was, Katie wasn't a fourth-grade girl anymore. She was Chef Pierre, the chocolate maker on board a giant cruise ship. It wasn't his fault Katie had turned into him. He shouldn't have to look like a fool. There was only one thing Katie could do: She was going to have to pick up one of those sharp knives and start carving.

Katie reached down and picked up the knife. She had never seen a knife quite that long or sharp before. She never would have been allowed to handle a knife like that—if she were still Katie. But she *wasn't* Katie anymore. She was Chef Pierre. He used knives all the time.

Katie chopped off a big chunk of chocolate from the top of the block.

Whoosh! The chocolate flew off the table and hit a woman in the face.

"Ouch!" the woman shouted.

"S-s-sorry!" Katie apologized. She gave the woman a nervous smile. "I guess you get to eat zee first bite of chocolate tonight."

A few people laughed. But the woman wasn't one of them.

Katie was surprised to hear her voice sound so deep. She was also surprised to discover she had a French accent. Of course, that sort of made sense since Chef Pierre was from France. Well, it made as much sense as anything did when the magic wind was around, anyway.

"Send a piece of chocolate over here," Dan shouted.

"Yeah," Stan added. "We want to start eating!"

Katie frowned. She knew how they felt. All

that yummy chocolate around and not a bite to eat yet. So Katie looked down at the big block of chocolate and thought about what a flying fish might look like.

Fish had round, smooth faces. Maybe she should start with that. Slowly, Katie began to carve the top of the chunk of chocolate into a rounder shape.

Or at least she tried to. But all she managed to do was hack off some chunks that flew off into the audience, hitting people.

"Hey! You just got chocolate on my new white dress!" a woman shouted out.

"Please step back," Katie said nervously.

Katie decided to forget about the head and work on the fish's tail instead.

"I weell carve zee tail now," she told the audience.

That didn't work out any better.

"This is stupid," Katie heard Suzanne say loudly. "I'm leaving."

"Wait for me," Lizzie told her.

Katie watched as Suzanne and Lizzie stormed out of the room. Lots of other passengers followed them.

But Katie kept carving. And chocolate kept flying.

"What are you trying to do, kill me?" a woman who got bopped between the eyes said.

Now that was ridiculous. Nobody had ever been killed from flying chocolate.

"What is going on here?"

Suddenly, Katie heard a loud voice bellowing from the back of the room. She looked up and saw the ship's captain heading right toward her. And boy, did he look angry.

He looked so mad that he made Katie forget that she was supposed to be a grown-up. Instead, she felt like a ten-year-old girl—a sad, scared, embarrassed ten-year-old girl.

So she did a very ten-year-old thing. "Zee demonstration eez over," she said. Then she dropped her knife and ran out of the room as fast as she could.

Katie ran and ran. She didn't want to see anyone. And she sure didn't want anyone to see her. She was crying really hard now. It was embarrassing to have people see you cry. Especially if they thought you were a famous chef from France.

Finally, Katie found an empty pantry in the back of the kitchen. There was no one there— just boxes and boxes of dry food. She ran inside and slammed the door shut. Then she sat on the floor and started to cry.

Suddenly Katie felt a cool breeze blowing on the back of her neck. She turned quickly to see if someone had opened the pantry door. But the door was shut tight.

The draft on Katie's neck grew colder. Her chef's hat blew off her head.

But the food on the shelves wasn't moving. The wind wasn't blowing on it. In fact, it wasn't blowing anywhere—except around Katie.

Which could only mean one thing: The magic wind was back!

The magic, wild tornado began blowing harder now, whipping around and around, faster and faster until . . .

It stopped. Just like that. The magic wind was gone. Katie Kazoo was back!

But so was the real Chef Pierre. And *ooh la la* was he confused!

Chapter 15

"What am I doing here?" Chef Pierre asked.
He shook his head and looked at Katie. "And
what are *you* doing here?"

"I . . . um . . . I took a wrong turn," Katie
told him. "I thought I was going to the arcade."

"Zee arcade eez on a different deck," Chef
Pierre said. "Zees eez zee baker's pantry. I never
go in zee baker's pantry. So why would I be
here now? I'm supposed to be . . ." He stopped
for a minute. "Oh right," he said sadly. "Now I
remember. I'm supposed to be carving my beeg
block of chocolate. But I messed zat up. I'm not
sure why. Eet eez all kind of foggy."

Katie didn't say anything. The truth was,

Chef Pierre hadn't messed anything up. *She* had. But she couldn't explain that to him. He'd never believe her. Katie wouldn't have believed it, either, if it hadn't just happened to her.

"I don't get eet," Chef Pierre said. "I was making a flying feesh. Zat eez zee easiest sculpture of all."

Katie frowned. It hadn't seemed easy to her.

"What a waste of dark chocolate," Chef Pierre continued. "Eet was one of my best batches ever."

"It's too bad no one will get the chance to taste it," Katie said. "It seems so sad that there's all this delicious chocolate, but no one can touch it."

Chef Pierre nodded. "I know what you mean," he agreed. "I love eating zee chocolate after I make eet. But the captain likes having zee statues around as decorations. Eet's just what zey do on zees ship." He sighed heavily. "Not zat eet matters anymore. I'm not going to be cooking, eating, or carving chocolate on zees ship. Not after zee mess I just made of zee demonstration."

Oh man. Now Katie felt even worse. Chef Pierre was probably going to be fired. And it was all her fault.

"Zee thing is, I really love zees job," Chef Pierre said sadly. "I get to make chocolate and travel all over zee world. Zee only thing I do not like eez carving in front of a crowd. I'm not a showman. I'm a chocolate chef."

"Maybe the captain won't be mad," Katie said. "Everybody can have a bad day, right?"

"Not on zees ship," Chef Pierre told her. "Zee captain doesn't tolerate any mistakes from anyone. Especially mistakes zat make zee passengers angry. And boy did I make zem angry."

"I think that woman overreacted," Katie told Chef Pierre. "You hit her with a piece of chocolate. I've never heard of chocolate seriously hurting anyone."

Chef Pierre laughed. "You're a funny child,"

he told her. "What eez your name?"

"Katie," she answered.

"Well, Katie," Chef Pierre said, "we'd better get you out of zees pantry. Passengers aren't supposed to be in here."

Katie stood up and followed Chef Pierre into the kitchen. She didn't want Chef Pierre getting into any more trouble because of her.

"There you are!"

Just then, the ship's captain came rushing into the kitchen.

"I've been looking all over for you," the captain said in his loud, booming voice.

"I am so sorry, sir," Chef Pierre said.

"Chocolate shouldn't be for showing," the captain explained. "It's for eating. Your show was a disaster. But everyone is raving about the delicious dark chocolate you made."

Katie and Chef Pierre looked curiously at the captain. What was he talking about?

"You mean zey are *eating* zee brick of carving chocolate?" Chef Pierre said. "Oh no. I shouldn't have just left eet sitting there."

"Actually, that was fine," the captain told him. "The people were eating it up as fast as they could get their hands on it."

"I love chocolate," Katie piped up. "And I've heard Chef Pierre's chocolate is the best! Especially his chocolate-covered strawberries . . ."

The captain looked down. It was the first time he even noticed Katie was standing there. "What are you doing in here, young lady?" he asked her.

"I . . . uh . . . I made a wrong turn," Katie said nervously. He was kind of a scary guy.

The captain shook his head. "You shouldn't be in the ship's galley. A girl your age shouldn't be around sharp knives and equipment."

Katie bit her lip and tried not to laugh. He didn't know the half of it.

The captain looked back at Pierre. "Are you aware that your performance upset several passengers? They claim they were injured."

"I know, sir," Pierre said. "I'll have my things

packed. I know zees is my last cruise."

"Wait. Maybe you don't have to fire Chef
Pierre," Katie said to the captain.

"Katie," Chef Pierre warned. "Not now."

The captain looked down at Katie. "That's
not for you to say, young lady."

"But I have a great idea," Katie told him.

The captain smiled. "I guess it won't hurt to listen to an idea."

"You don't have a candy shop on the Promenade Deck," Katie told him. "And every mall needs a candy shop. Back in Cherrydale, we have this place called Cinnamon's Candy Shop, and all the kids love it. Why can't you have a chocolate shop on board?"

"A chocolate shop," Chef Pierre said. "Zat has always been my dream."

"You could make and sell chocolate," Katie told him. "And you wouldn't have to put on a show."

The captain thought for a moment. "That's not a bad idea," he said.

"I could make chocolate bars in zee shape of zee ship," Chef Pierre suggested. "And, of course, small fish, mermaids, and dolphins."

"And chocolate-covered strawberries," Katie suggested.

"It's worth a try," the captain agreed. "Your chocolate *is* awfully good."

"*Merci*, sir," Chef Pierre said.

"Thank Katie," the captain told him. "After all, it was her great idea."

Chapter 16

"Where is everyone?" Katie asked Lori the next morning when she arrived at the Cruisin' Kids Clubhouse. She was the only kid there.

"I was just about to ask you the same thing," Lori said. "Aren't Suzanne and Lizzie with you?"

Katie shook her head. "My family ate breakfast in our cabin," she said. "I thought Suzanne would be here before me."

"None of the Minnows are here," Lori said. "The other groups have already left to go to their activities. I was waiting for you guys. I thought we could play a game of volleyball by the pool this morning."

Katie frowned. Volleyball was one of those

things you couldn't really do all by yourself.

She looked out the window at the pool below. She couldn't believe her eyes. There, right by the snack bar, were the other Minnows. They were standing in a circle. In the middle stood Suzanne. She was holding a big sign. It said:

"Um, Lori?" Katie pointed to the Pool Deck below. "I think I found them."

Lori followed Katie's gaze. She spotted Suzanne and the other kids. "What is she doing?" Lori asked Katie.

"It looks like she started her own camp," Katie told her.

"She can't do that," Lori said.

Katie sighed. Lori didn't know Suzanne very well. But Katie did. Suzanne did whatever she wanted, whenever she wanted, wherever she wanted. From the looks of things, what Suzanne wanted to do now was to start her own camp.

Katie turned and headed for the door.

"Now where are *you* going?" Lori asked her.

"To talk to Suzanne," Katie said.

"Wait up," Lori said. "I'm going with you."

✳ ✳ ✳

A few seconds later, Katie and Lori had joined the Minnows on the Pool Deck.

"Sorry," Suzanne told Lori. "This club is for kids only."

"I'm a kid," Katie told her.

"Well, I guess you can join," Suzanne said. "But you should know this club is really different from the other one. For one thing, we don't climb rock walls, we don't have relay races, and we *definitely* don't play wall ball."

"What do you do?" Lori asked her.

Suzanne held out her wrist. She was wearing a purple bracelet that was made from construction paper. "Well, for one thing, we don't wear green wristbands. We wear purple. It's a much cooler color."

"Okay," Lori said. "But what activities are you going to do?"

"Right now we're hanging out on the Pool Deck," Suzanne told her.

"That's an *activity*?" Katie asked.

Suzanne shrugged. "Sure. Why not?" she said. "And later we're going to hang out in the library. After that we're going to hang out in the karaoke café."

"The karaoke café is only open to adults," Lori reminded her.

"Oh," Suzanne said. "Well, then we'll hang out *outside* the karaoke café."

"That sounds like lots of fun," Lizzie said. "I've been to a karaoke café at home, but

I've never been outside of one. You have the greatest ideas, Suzanne."

Katie figured Lizzie would do whatever Suzanne told her to. And Carly just wanted to be with the other girls. But she couldn't figure out how Suzanne had gotten Stan and Dan to be part of her club.

"I don't get it. Why would you want to be in Suzanne's club instead of the Cruisin' Kids Club?" she asked the twins.

Before Stan or Dan could answer, Suzanne opened her mouth. "They're bored with doing the same activities on every cruise. My activities are cooler."

"We have done all the rock climbing and ice-skating a million times before," Stan said.

"Yeah, there's nothing new," Dan added. "We thought we'd give this a shot."

"But isn't just hanging out boring?" Lori asked them.

"No," Suzanne butted in. "Because they're hanging out with me. And I'm *never* boring."

She looked at Katie. "We're going to hang out on the other side of the Pool Deck now. Are you coming?"

Katie glanced over at Lori. She looked very sad. Katie couldn't leave her all alone. And besides, doing nothing but hanging out actually seemed *un*cool to her.

"No, thanks," she said. "I'll see you at dinner."

"Suit yourself," Suzanne said. Then she turned and led the other Minnows across the deck to a row of deck chairs. "This is going to be a completely different kind of hanging out," she told them.

"Definitely," Katie could hear Lizzie agreeing. "This side of the pool has green and white lounge chairs. But that side has blue and white chairs. That's *completely* different."

"Well, not completely," Carly said. "Because green and blue are in the same family. Green is actually blue and yellow mixed. The *kind* of green is based on how much blue and how much yellow you use and . . ." Carly's voice faded into the background as she and the other kids walked away.

"The captain is not going to be happy," Lori told Katie as they watched the kids leave. "He doesn't want mutiny on board his ship."

Katie gasped. A mutiny. Wow! That sounded like something that only happened on pirate ships. Suzanne had done some pretty incredible things, but this just might have been the most incredible.

There was a mutiny on the high seas. And Suzanne Lock had started it all.

Chapter 17

"Well, Katie, I guess it's just you and me today," Lori told her as they walked back into the Cruisin' Kids Clubhouse together.

Katie frowned. The whole point of going on this cruise with Suzanne's family was so she would have a friend to hang out with instead of just being with grown-ups all day. But Lori was a grown-up. A nice grown-up, but a grown-up just the same.

But Katie wasn't going to leave. Lori looked so sad. And worried. Not that Katie blamed her. A mutiny was a pretty huge deal.

"Is there anything special you would really like to do?" Lori asked her. "Maybe something on the ship you haven't tried yet?"

Katie thought about that. She'd been on the waterslide, played miniature golf, climbed the rock wall, and shot hoops. Just about the only thing she hadn't done was go shopping on the Promenade Deck.

Suddenly Katie got another one of her great ideas. "That's it!" she exclaimed excitedly.

"What's *it*?" Lori asked curiously.

"I know what we can do," she said. "And it's something even Suzanne won't be able to resist."

"What is it?" Lori asked excitedly.

"I'll show you," Katie told her as she headed for the door. "We need to go to the Promenade Deck."

"We're going shopping?" Lori asked. She sounded confused.

"No," Katie assured her. "This is something much better."

An hour later, the Minnows were all gathered on the Promenade Deck—together. They were inside the Cruising Clothes Boutique. Each one of them was wearing a cool outfit from the store.

"See, I told you my club would do the coolest stuff ever," Suzanne said to Katie. "And now we're having a fashion show." She tipped the brim of her purple sun hat over one eye and straightened the skirt of the purple-and-white sundress she would be modeling in the show.

Katie shook her head. Suzanne was unbelievable. For one thing, it hadn't been Suzanne's idea to put on a kids' fashion show to advertise clothes sold on board the ship. It had been Katie's. And it was the Cruisin' Kids Club putting on the show, not Suzanne's club.

But there was no point in telling Suzanne that. It was easier to let her think she'd planned the whole thing. What was important was that the kids were all having fun—*together*. And they were. Even the boys! Lori looked so happy.

She winked at Katie and gave her a thumbs-up.

"So all we have to do is walk outside to the end of that road thing?" Stan asked Suzanne.

"It's called a runway," Suzanne said. "And you don't just walk. You do a *model* walk. Like this." Suzanne began prancing around the store, lifting her knees up high and stretching her legs out as she walked. She looked like a purple-and-white pony.

Lizzie began to giggle.

Suzanne stopped and glared at her. "What's so funny?"

"Oh, you mean you were serious?" Lizzie said. She gulped. "I'm sorry. I thought you were just goofing around."

"I never joke about modeling," Suzanne told her.

"Of course," Lizzie said nervously. She began to walk around the store, lifting her legs up high and stretching them out, just like Suzanne had. "Is this right?"

"It's better," Suzanne said. "And don't forget

to turn around a few times so people can see your bathing suit cover-up from all the angles."

Lizzie pranced around the store and turned around and around like a pinwheel. "Oooh, I'm getting dizzy," she said.

Carly spun around, too. Suddenly, she lost her balance and wound up falling into a rack of clothes. Katie raced over to help her up.

"Don't worry," Carly said from beneath the pile of blouses and bathing suits. "I'm okay. Maybe I'll just do the walking, not the spinning," she added.

"Me too," Lizzie said. "I'm pretty good at the walking part." She started prancing around the store again.

"There's no way I'm doing that," Dan told Suzanne.

"Me neither," Stan said.

Suzanne looked really mad. "You have to. This is a fashion show. That's a fashion show walk." Then she groaned. "Oh, what's the point? This is never going to work."

Uh-oh. It looked like Suzanne was about to storm out of the shop. Katie had to do something.

"Don't some fashion shows have dancers?" she asked Suzanne nervously.

Suzanne shrugged. "I guess so. Why?"

"Do you guys dance?" Katie asked the twins.

"No," both brothers said at the same time.

"But I can walk on my hands," Stan said.

"Then you should do that," Katie told him. "And, Dan, you can walk right next to him the regular way."

"Why would they do that?" Suzanne demanded.

"Um . . . er . . . because . . ." Katie stammered. She looked over at the twins. They were both wearing the same beach outfit—a green-and-yellow flowered bathing suit with a yellow shirt and green flip-flops. "Um . . . because that way they can show the same outfit from two different angles."

Suzanne thought about that for a minute. "That will work," she said. "Besides, it won't matter. After everyone sees me in this sundress and hat, they won't be able to think about anything else."

Chapter 18

"Did you all have a wonderful time on your cruise?" Lori asked Katie's and Suzanne's families as they got ready to leave the ship the next morning. The boat had docked overnight, and now it was time to go home.

"I can't believe how fast five days went," Katie's father told her as he began rolling his suitcase down toward the gangway of the ship. "It seems like just yesterday you were saying hi to us instead of good-bye."

"It was fun," Katie's mother said. "I feel so rested."

Katie looked down. She was wearing her green Minnow wristband, the medal she'd gotten from the magician, and a T-shirt that said MY NEW BEST FRIEND IS A DOLPHIN. "This was the best vacation ever!" she exclaimed.

"It was fun," Suzanne agreed.

Katie smiled at Suzanne. Ever since the modeling show, Suzanne had been a whole lot nicer. She had just needed an activity that she was really good at. Katie didn't blame her. She understood that it was important to feel like you were the best at something every now and then. And it was especially important to Suzanne.

Suzanne reached up and touched her new purple sun hat. "Thanks for buying the outfit I modeled in the show, Mom."

Mrs. Lock grinned. "I couldn't resist it. You looked so pretty."

"Suzanne, pretty," Heather said. "Very pretty."

Suzanne smiled at her sister for the first time the whole cruise. "She's getting smarter," she told her parents.

Everybody laughed.

Just then, someone came racing through the ship's lobby. "Katie! Wait!" he shouted.

Katie turned around just in time to see Chef Pierre coming toward her. He was carrying a big, white box.

"I'm so glad I caught you," he said. "I made zees chocolates especially for you."

"Oh wow!" Katie exclaimed.

"I created a mold in zee shape of zees ship. And I made white chocolate–covered strawberries. I know chocolate-covered strawberries are your favorite."

"Thank you so much," Katie said. "I bet your new shop is going to be the busiest one on the whole Promenade Deck."

"I should get back to making more chocolate," Chef Pierre said. "Zee new passengers will be boarding zees afternoon. *Merci* for everything, Katie."

"You're really welcome," Katie told him.

"What was that all about?" Suzanne asked

as Chef Pierre walked away. "How come we all didn't get a box of chocolates?"

"Don't worry, I'll share them," Katie assured her.

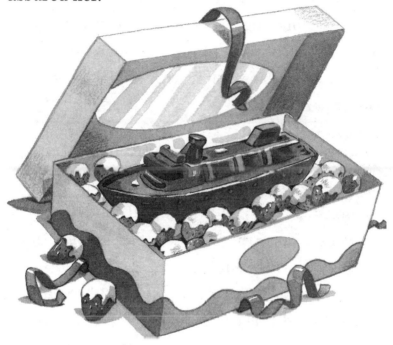

"Me too!" Heather said. "Me too!"

Suzanne rolled her eyes. "Maybe her name should be Me Too."

"She just wants to be like you," Suzanne's dad said.

Suzanne sighed. "I guess I can't blame her for that," she said. "A lot of people want to be like me."

Now Lizzie came racing over. She gave Suzanne a big hug. "I am so glad you were on this cruise," she said. "I had so much fun. And I promise to keep practicing my model walk until I get it perfect."

Suzanne smiled. "That will take a lot of practice," she told her.

"I know," Lizzie said. "I don't expect to be as wonderful as you right away. But I'm trying."

Oh boy, Katie thought. *Heather isn't the only one who should be nicknamed Me Too.*

"Okay, everyone, time to leave and go back to real life," Katie's dad said.

Katie followed him to a taxi stand. It would be nighttime before they were back in Cherrydale. It was great to go on vacation, but it would be great to be home again, too.

Just then, Katie felt a cool breeze blowing on the back of her neck. She gulped. Oh no!

Had the magic wind come back again? Already? Was it going to switcheroo her into someone else—right here in front of everyone?

"Whoa!" Suzanne shouted suddenly. "That wind almost blew my new hat off!"

Katie grinned. If Suzanne felt the wind, then it couldn't be the magic wind. It was just an ordinary, everyday kind of wind. The kind of wind that didn't switcheroo her into someone else. And that was great. Because that meant Katie would stay Katie—at least for now.

And there wasn't anyone she'd rather be.

About the Author

Nancy Krulik is the author of more than 150 books for children and young adults, including three *New York Times* best sellers. She lives in New York City with her husband, composer Daniel Burwasser, and their children, Amanda and Ian. When she's not busy writing the *Katie Kazoo, Switcheroo* series, Nancy loves swimming, reading, and going to the movies.

About the Illustrators

John & Wendy have illustrated all of the *Katie Kazoo* books, but when they're not busy drawing Katie and her friends, they like to paint, take photographs, travel, and play music in their rock 'n' roll band. They live and work in Brooklyn, New York.